The Lighthouse Keeper's Tea

Ronda and David Armitage

Scholastic Children's Books,
Commonwealth House, 1-19 New Oxford Street,
London WC1A 1NU, UK
a division of Scholastic Ltd
London ~ New York ~ Toronto ~ Sydney ~ Auckland
Mexico City ~ New Delhi ~ Hong Kong

First published in hardback by Scholastic Ltd, 2001
This paperback edition published by Scholastic Ltd, 2002

ISBN 0 439 97938 2

Printed and bound in China
All rights reserved

2 4 6 8 10 9 7 5 3

Mr and Mrs Grinling lived with their cat, Hamish, and his family in a little white house perched high on the cliff.

Some days Mr Grinling was the lighthouse keeper, but other days he just got in Mrs Grinling's way.

"Mr G, Mr G, you're always under my feet," complained Mrs Grinling.

Mr Grinling sighed. "I'm bored, Mrs G. Now that Sam helps at the lighthouse I haven't got enough to do."

"A new pastime," said Mrs Grinling, "that's what you need. What do you enjoy doing?"

"Eating?" suggested Mr Grinling. He dipped his finger in the icing. "That's it," he said, "the perfect pastime, if I like eating I'm sure I'd like cooking."

Mrs Grinling looked alarmed. "Perhaps I could help?"

"No, thank you," said Mr Grinling. "I can do it myself. You have a little rest while I make some bread for our lunch. Just pop in these ingredients, mix them about a bit and hey presto, the bread will be ready in no time."

The bread rose and
rose and...

flopped.

When Mr Grinling tried
to put it in the oven the
dough slithered
everywhere.
"I don't like cooking,"
he decided. "Much
too messy."

"Oh dear, such a pity," said Mrs Grinling. "Perhaps something outdoors would suit you better. What about birdwatching with your telescope?"

"Good idea, Mrs G," agreed Mr Grinling. "I could keep an eye on those pesky seagulls."

So he packed a little something and set out.

"Here's your warm jumper," Mrs Grinling called after him.

"No, thank you," replied Mr Grinling. "It's a beautiful day, look at that sun."

He didn't see any seagulls, but he did spy

 five greenfinches,

four mistle thrushes,

 three mallard ducks,

two black swans

and a kingfisher on the river bank.

"I'm enjoying this," thought Mr Grinling.

"A nice change from seagulls."

It was during lunch that he remembered that he didn't like . . .

. . . cows.

"Shoo," he said bravely.
"Moo," mooed the
gentle cows.

Mr Grinling scrambled
up the tree while the cows
finished his cheese, lettuce
and tomato sandwiches.

He rang Sam.
 "Help, help, I'm sure
I've just seen a
dangerous wild boar."
 Sam was surprised.
 "A wild boar?"
 "Ferocious," said
 Mr Grinling.

"And I'm very cold. Please
rescue me."
 "Where are you?" asked Sam.
 "Well," explained Mr Grinling.
"I'm up a very thin tree, in a
field, surrounded by a green
hedge and a few cows."

It took Sam several hours to find him.
"No more birdwatching," said
Mr Grinling. "Far too dangerous
with all those wild . . . "
"Cows?" said Sam helpfully.

But Mr Grinling was still bored. "Oh dear," he thought. "There must be something I enjoy."

He tried the violin, but that was too screechy for everyone.

He went out with his kite, but that was too windy.

And then there was the roller blading, but that was an absolute disaster.

"Perhaps old dogs can't learn new tricks," teased Mrs Grinling.

"Old," spluttered Mr Grinling. "Did you say old? Sea dogs like me are never too old to learn new tricks, I just haven't found the perfect one yet."

"M-m-m," said Mrs Grinling.

One morning in Wild Horses Bay, Mr Grinling met Sam carrying a large board. He was surprised. "I didn't know you were a surfer, Sam."

"One of the best," boasted Sam and he rode the big waves while Mr Grinling watched.

"I wish I could do that," said Mr Grinling.

"Come and have a go," called Sam.

He pulled Mr Grinling onto the surfboard.

"There might be a bit of a problem," Mr Grinling tried to explain, but Sam didn't hear him.

Mr Grinling stood up on the surfboard . . .

. . . and he fell off the surfboard.

"Swim," shouted Sam.

"Glug, glug," glugged Mr Grinling.

"I can't," he spluttered. "That's the bit of a problem."

"Huh-huh," Sam shook his head. "If you want to be a surfer, that's not a bit of a problem, that's an enormous problem."

"I'm an extremely good floater," said Mr Grinling hopefully.

Sam was firm. "If you can't swim, you can't be a surfer."

But Mr Grinling had made up his mind. Surfing was what he wanted to do most in the world.

"Don't breathe a word to Mrs G," said Mr Grinling. "She thinks old dogs can't learn new tricks. I'll show her that this one can."

"Shall I help you with the swimming?" asked Sam.

"No, thank you," said Mr Grinling. "I know exactly what to do."

He found a rock in just the right place and lowered himself into the water.

"I splash with my arms like this...

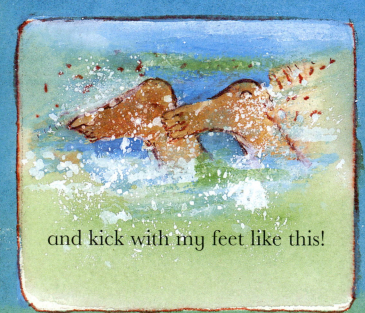

and kick with my feet like this!

And then I do both together..."

"Glug, glug," glugged Mr Grinling and he splashed wildly.

"Help, help," cried Mr Grinling, "I'm drowning."

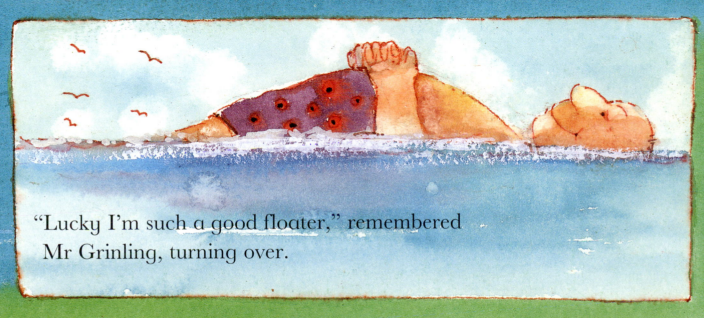

"Lucky I'm such a good floater," remembered Mr Grinling, turning over.

He floated around the old jetty
and through the Needles. He
floated beside the white sand
beach and over the wreck of the
Hesperus. He floated across the
channel rippling with irritable
little waves.

He floated past the lighthouse and the little white house.
   At last he floated up onto the beach.

"Perhaps I do need a little bit of help," he whispered to Hamish as he crept to bed.

JOIN TODAY said the notice at the Green Lagoon Pool.

"I've come to learn to swim," said Mr Grinling.

"We've got just the class for you," replied the swimming instructor. "First we'll try the kicking."

"Glug, glug," glugged Mr Grinling and he sank to the bottom of the pool.

"Now we'll use our arms," called the instructor.

"Splash, splash," splashed Mr Grinling, but he still sank.

The children watched.

"We'll help you, Mr Grinling," they said and they did.

GREEN LAGOON
• Beginner's Class •

Soon he could
dog paddle,

freestyle,

backstroke,

and butterfly.

"Congratulations," said the swimming
instructor. "I always say you're never
too old to learn."

"Well done," exclaimed Sam.
"Now I'll show you how to surf."
  "No, thank you," said Mr Grinling.
"I'll do it myself."
  "Stubborn old sea dog,"
said Sam quietly.

Mr Grinling bought a bright yellow wetsuit and a shiny red
surfboard. Every day he practised where he thought no one could
see him and every day he fell into the water hundreds of times.
  "One thousand and one," muttered Mr Grinling as he
scrambled onto the board again.

Seven shark fins rose in the water.
"Blither my whiskers!" shouted Mr Grinling.

Seven sharks surfed beside him.
Mr Grinling stayed on the surfboard all the way to the shallows.

Seven sharks climbed out of the water.
 "Well," cried Sam, "our shark trick certainly
helped an old sea dog learn his new trick."
 "You frightened the life out of me,"
said Mr Grinling, but a grin
stretched right across
his face.

It wasn't long before
Mr Grinling could ride the
waves just like a real surfer.
"Now I can show Mrs
Grinling," he announced.
"Not yet, not yet," begged
the children. "We've thought
of the perfect occasion."

On the day of the Wild Horse Bay Sea Carnival, Mrs Grinling searched high and low for Mr Grinling. "I don't understand. He always enters the sandcastle competition and runs in the sack race. Whatever's happened to him? Wherever can he be?" she asked the children.

"Don't worry," they said and they arranged a deck chair for her.
"So you can get a better view of the surfing," they explained.
And they all lined up at the water's edge.
As the big wave rose up across the bay the drums began to roll.
Mrs Grinling watched the little round figure on the surfboard.

"Such daring," she exclaimed.

"Amazing," she cheered.

"Extraordinary," she gasped.

The figure in yellow surfed almost to her feet.

He peeled off his wetsuit and bowed. "I'd like you to meet an old sea dog," he said.

Mrs Grinling was speechless.

She gave Mr Grinling a great big hug. "I did it all by myself," he said proudly. "With a little bit of help from Sam and the children."

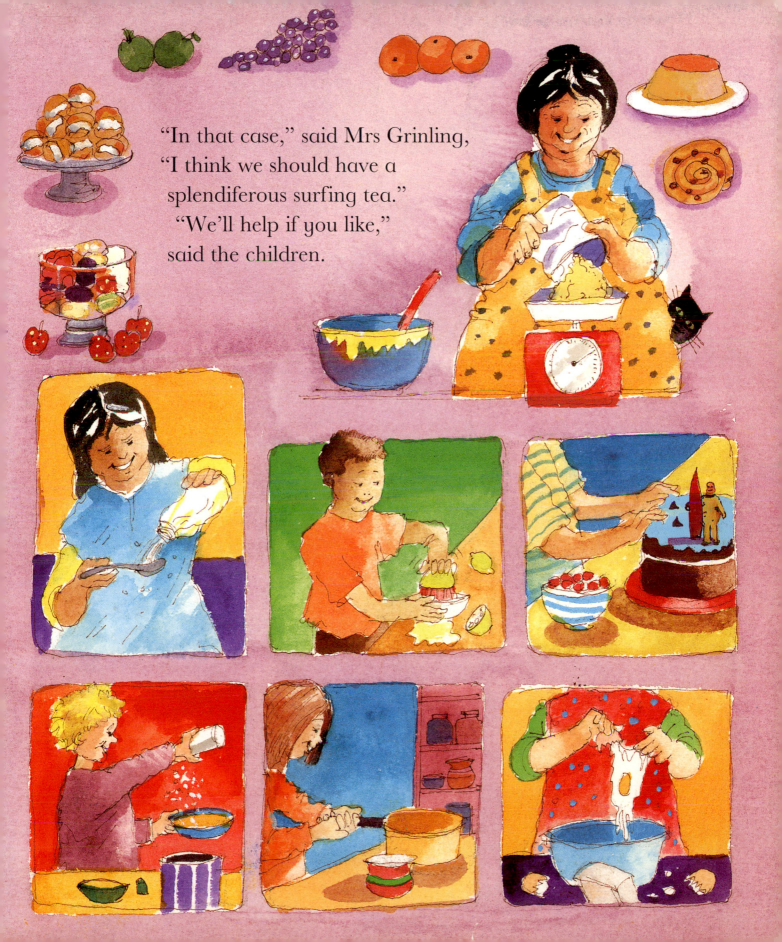

"In that case," said Mrs Grinling,
"I think we should have a
splendiferous surfing tea."
"We'll help if you like,"
said the children.